The Miniaturisation of Sheila Trinket

Cath Barton

ARROYO SECO PRESS

Logo by Morgan G Robles

Editor: LeAnne Hunt

Arroyo Seco Press

www.arroyosecopress.org

Cover art: image BWFolsom from iStock

ISBN: 979-8-9918724-2-3

To all those people who feel
smaller than they really are–
may this inspire them to fly!

Contents

Premonition

Sheila had never told Ted. He would have laughed at her, possibly worse; being a rat-catcher he was a down-to-earth person, not interested in the fanciful. And he would definitely have considered this fanciful.

Sheila's experience of meeting her future self in miniaturised form occurred during the early days of her married life, when she and Ted partied often, long and hard, careless of the consequences. It happened one morning when she was bleary-eyed after such a night, so not entirely sure she wasn't just seeing things. Especially as the miniature future Sheila spoke in a very high-pitched and not very comprehensible way.

'You look–' Sheila started. She blinked; yes, there really was a small creature speaking to her from a high shelf in her kitchen. 'You look like me. Only older. And smaller. Obviously smaller.' She giggled, and her small future self frowned before exploding into a tirade of swear words. Sheila shrugged, made herself a cup of strong black coffee and took it into the living room. This was in the days before she and Ted had dogs; the living room was quiet.

Apart from the small future her in the kitchen, everything seemed normal. Though, alarmingly, the little her was still up there later, on the shelf of mugs they kept as spares, when she heard Ted slamming the front door. Sheila was chopping veg for their supper. She waved the knife at the creature – 'Time to go,' she said in as strong a voice as she could muster. And that was it, pff! One minute there was a little future Sheila, next nothing. Not even a space on the shelf.

Sheila remembered that strange happening now and again, over the years, but she was not one for portents or omens – good or bad – so she didn't dwell on it, and when things played out as they did, it was Ted who was affected rather more than her.

On the shelf

Like so many couples, Ted and Sheila Trinket rubbed along together in spite of their differences; they had found ways of accommodating one another's annoying habits and did not expect, after twenty years of marriage, that anything was going to change radically between them.

Ted had his work, and his evenings in the snug of The Square Hole with his drinking buddies; Sheila was quite content watching quizzes on TV on a Monday night, cookery programmes on other nights, and doing her embroidery and knitting. They had two dogs, or rather, Ted had his terrier Mincer, who went out with him every day, and Sheila had ManyBucks, an elderly and rather malodorous boxer, who settled down by her side every evening, gently snoring.

There was really no warning of what happened – it came like a change in the weather, though whereas a change from summer warmth to autumn chill in the mornings was normal and unremarkable, what happened to Sheila was most definitely not.

One morning, Ted woke, turned over and put out a hand to Sheila, only to find that her side of the bed was empty and cold. He stretched, scratched, rolled out of bed, pulled on his dressing gown and stumbled downstairs and into the kitchen. Mincer danced round his feet as usual, but ManyBucks was asleep in his basket and there was no sign of Sheila. Ted picked up the kettle, carried it over to the sink and started to fill it. As he did so, he heard a high-pitched sound. He turned off the tap and wheeled round, looking for the source of the noise. But it had stopped. He turned on the tap again and resumed his filling of the kettle. The noise resumed too, louder this time. Off with the tap again, but this time what he now recognised as a kind of squealing continued. And he could see where it was coming from – the mouth of his wife who, somehow shrunk to a miniature version of herself, was sitting on a high shelf, next to their best glasses, one of which she was now tapping with her tiny wedding ring. She was, Ted thought, turning an unhealthy colour as she mouthed what was clearly extreme displeasure.

'What the blazes? Are you alright, Sheila?'

Of course she was not alright, he knew that, but he was, as he told his mates in The Square Hole later, nonplussed.

2

'I mean,' he told Mike and Dave and everyone else who was there, 'nothing like that has ever happened to us before.'

What happened next was even more unexpected. 'She took off,' he said, flapping his arms in imitation of a bird, 'just like that. Took off and did two complete circuits of the kitchen. I was gobsmacked. I mean,' he said, 'wouldn't you be?'

'What did you do then, mate?' said one or other of the men in the pub.

'What did I do? I dunno. Probably said something inane like "You can fly", which was, of course, obvious. Then I opened the door, she flew out and down the street, and I made myself a cup of tea, like I'd been trying to do before she started her squealing about me putting too much water in the kettle. Well, that's what I assumed she was trying to say. Anyway, what would any of you have done?'

No-one had an answer. Ted was to discover, in the days that followed, that there were many questions to which no-one could give him an answer.

Putting the word out

Missing, presumed lost: Miniature woman (aged 58). Answers to name Sheila. Dark frizzy hair. Ruddy complexion. Wears spectacles. Distinguishing feature: no little finger on left hand.

Escaped from home in Hangar Lane, Enfield, on morning of Friday, 13th September, 2016. Thought to be still in the Enfield area.

Likely to be seen flying – could be mistaken for large bee or wasp. Keep windows closed and, if seen, approach with caution. Protective clothing recommended if trying to detain her.

Substantial reward for safe return, no questions asked.

Please contact Ted Trinket (husband) c/o The Square Hole, Market Street, Enfield, evenings between 8 and 10pm.

Miles and miles away

Reports came flooding in. She was spotted in the hairdressers, the launderette, the social club, the church – church? Sheila never went to church, Ted knew that one couldn't be true. Or was it? He found it difficult to know what was true any more. What were reported as sightings of tiny Sheila, reports of her buzzing around like an angry bee, might have been just that, sightings of an angry bee. Except bees didn't wear spectacles, or long black skirts. Though some of them had frizzy hair. Ted had been researching bees, and there were some that looked remarkably like people with frizzy hair. And had black bodies. Perhaps Sheila had been turned into a bee? And she might not have been wearing her specs when it happened. Or they could have fallen off.

Ted found it all very tiring. Just thinking about it was tiring. Plus the phone ringing all the time, with the next sighting (the pub having given out his number), and also with people who needed his services; rats didn't disappear just because your wife had, and people could get very shirty. Of course it was stressful, having rats in your house; he knew that.

'I'm sorry,' he said, 'but my wife– look, I'm really sorry…' He told people he'd get back to them, but he didn't, and after a bit they gave up.

Now he was worried about the rats as well as about Sheila. They wouldn't just go away, and he was the last rat-catcher left in Enfield. He was worried about worrying too; it wasn't good for his blood pressure.

It was a Thursday morning when the call came from Iltringham.

'Where did you say?'

Ted had never heard of Iltringham. He looked it up online. The first place he found was in Australia. That had to be wrong. Birds might fly to Africa, but they surely didn't go as far as Australia, and neither did bees. There was no way tiny Sheila could be there. He searched again and sure enough, there was an Iltringham in England. Miles away from Enfield though. Miles and miles. But the person on the phone had captured her, had her under a jam jar, buzzing and jumping.

'When can you get here? I don't like to leave it, but I can't stay in all day.'

'It's not an it.' Ted heard the way he must have sounded to the man. Pathetic. He felt pathetic. 'It's my wife.'

'I know, guv, that's why I'm ringing you. I do appreciate that—' the man hesitated, then cleared his throat before continuing in a rush. 'Any road, she sounds pretty mad at you, so you'd better come and sort things out.'

Ted got his terrier into the car. ManyBucks would have to stay at home. He went into the living room, the room where Sheila always sat with the boxer by her side. The depression was still there on the sofa. Now there was a depression in the dog bed too. No ManyBucks there. No ManyBucks in his basket in the kitchen either. Nothing, not even a residual smell. Ted swallowed hard, pushing down the panic rising in his stomach at the thought of what Sheila would say if anything bad had happened to her dog. He told himself not to worry; ManyBucks had to be somewhere. He, Ted, had to focus on getting to Iltringham, though he had no idea what he would do when he got there.

'Just drive,' he said to himself. He drove, comforted by the presence of Mincer by his side. A dog, he thought to himself, is so much easier than a wife. But, for all that, he was missing Sheila.

Her secret that wasn't secret

Although Sheila had never told her husband about the fact that she had met her future self, miniaturised on the kitchen shelf, there was something else she had not managed to keep secret from him.

In the third year of their marriage, after the first glory days had faded, and routine was something with which she did not yet feel comfortable– she was only 25, for goodness sake! – Sheila embarked on an amorous adventure. It was with the milkman. At the time Ted was working for a pest control company, and had regular office hours. The milkman, whose name was Derek, would come round to the back door after his round. He brought the occasional extra pint, but Sheila asked him not to do that in case Ted smelled a rat.

'Ha, ha, notice what I said there,' she giggled. 'Smelled a rat, and him a ratcatcher!'

'Stop talking, darling,' said Derek.

He said a few other things, things that Ted never said. And did things Ted never did.

'What if your hubby comes home early?' he said.

'He never comes home early,' said Sheila. And Ted never did. But he heard talk, because Enfield wasn't a big place, and Derek had form, Sheila not being by any means the first woman in whom he'd taken an interest. Ted used to drink in a pub called The Snake and Rattle at that time. After he heard the gossip he stopped going there. It made him feel sick, the idea that he was being cuckolded.

When Sheila said she wanted a dog for company Ted knew things must be over with Derek; it was a relief. Why she wanted a boxer he didn't ask. She had a succession of them after that; they were all lazy and smelly.

The way things were (1)

'That dog needs a bath,' Ted said to his wife, wrinkling his nose as he plonked himself down in his chair.

'So do you, sweet pie,' Sheila said. 'You whiff something rotten.'

'I 'spect I do. Five dead ones today, well niffy they were. Give a bloke a break though. Let me drink me cup of tea and then I'll get out of these clothes.'

Time was Sheila would have been glad to help him out of his clothes, and vice versa. But age, if it hadn't exactly withered them, had reduced the urges of the flesh. Sheila wriggled down in her chair. Next to her the ever-faithful hound ManyBucks farted loudly.

'Chrissakes, Sheila. You gotta do something about him!' Ted put out a toe towards the boxer.

'Watch out, he'll nip you,' Sheila said.

They carried on in this fashion, exchanging their usual banter, as the daylight dimmed.

That was how things were between them, before.

The way things were (2)

It was broken again. ManyBucks did it, or so Ted said. Sheila blamed Mincer. Either way, the back door had fallen off its hinges and wouldn't shut properly. A gusty wind was blowing dead leaves in from the garden, and the kitchen floor was littered with them.

'Get it swept,' Sheila ordered her husband.

'Why me?' he said. 'Your dog did it.'

'Wrong.'

They argued in this way, back and forth, for some time. Meanwhile the two dogs were standing looking at them. Mincer, keen to get going, started to whine.

'Where's the back door key?' said Ted.

'What's got into you? We can't lock it!'

'True, but I never understand why you have to be so secretive about where you put the key!'

'Oh, for goodness sake, Ted Trinket. We do possess more than one key. You should be able to find one of them. Except, as I say–'

'Enough, woman.'

Mincer was bending backwards now, as if he was doing a limbo dance.

'You better take that dog and get out of my hair. Go and see that man you know who can fix most anything. If you would be so kind.' With which retort Sheila shuffled off into the sitting-room, followed, slowly, by ManyBucks, who farted loudly, emitting a noxious smell.

This was in the previous times, when Ted thought he knew the worst of everything, and drowning his sorrows several nights a week in The Square Hole worked for him. Now, as he drove towards Iltringham, stone-cold sober, he realised that he knew nothing, and he thought for the first time in years about that milkman with whom Sheila had an affair. He'd never confronted her about it. Hadn't wanted to know any more than he'd heard from the gossipmongers. Any more than he wanted to know what was going on now. But there was no getting away from it.

No-one there

The man in Iltringham was half-apologetic.

'Just bad luck,' he said. 'One minute it was there, the next something blew the jar over and it was gone. Out the window.'

'Bad luck?! Bloody careless, more like! Why the hell did you have the window open? And it's not an it, it's my wife, like I already told you.'

'Keep your hair on mate. I didn't need to call you, did I. You were lucky I even heard about it.'

The man was squirming a bit, embarrassed now. Mincer was straining on his lease and whining. 'You better keep that dog off me,' the man said, backing away.

'Okay, okay, he ain't going to hurt you. It's rats he wants.'

'Rats? What the– '

'Don't worry, we're off. Thank you for nothing.'

Ted slammed his car door as he got in, and Mincer whined more loudly.

'Whoa, boy. We're heading home.'

Smelling a rat

Ted was tired, and he wanted a drink. But halfway home he got a call.

'Nice little job, Mincer,' he said to his dog. 'Let's do it.'

The house was on a corner. And all in darkness. But he had been told to call, 'whatever the time', so he rang the doorbell. Nothing stirred. He walked down the side passage, and round to the back door. It was slightly ajar so he gave it an experimental push, but there was something behind it stopping it opening further. Mincer, who had been quiet until then, set up with the noise which meant they had found their target – the low rumble in the throat which meant they had found a rat.

Dispatching the rat was easy; dealing with the other body behind the door was more problematic, especially as this was meant to be just a quick job before they headed to The Square Hole for a restorative snifter. Or several.

Sheila, back

'Someone is dead. Even the trees know it...'

Ted could hear the singing as he opened the front door. It was high and off-key. He could make out little of the words, and what he could hear didn't make any sense. In the living room Sheila's chair was still empty and cold, though ManyBucks was back from wherever he'd disappeared to, curled up asleep in his bed. Ted was feeling queasy after all the whisky he'd drunk; the cold air had done nothing to sober him up. He could not face what he might find in the kitchen, staggered up the stairs and made it into the bathroom just in time.

'Ted Trinket, you are a godforsaken mess.' He lifted his head from the toilet bowl to see his wife standing in the doorway. Full-size Sheila.

'You're back to normal,' he managed to say after a few minutes.

'I've never been anything other than normal,' Sheila said.

'So, how do you explain–' Ted turned back to the toilet as another stream of vomit erupted from his innards.

'You're the one who needs to do the explaining. I'm going back to bed now I know I don't need to send out a search party for you.' She swung round without waiting for Ted to respond.

The body in the park

Sheila was home, back to her normal size and shape, but changed in ways neither she nor Ted understood. They'd picked up as they'd left off – what else could they do? – but both of them were on edge. Sheila had no memory of being small, which troubled her when Ted told her the story.

'I don't know whether or not I enjoyed it,' she said.

'You didn't sound as if you did at the time,' Ted said. 'You sounded angry.' He couldn't help wondering whether Sheila would fly off again.

And then there was the body issue.

It was now late autumn, dark evenings and bad weather making everything seem worse. A threatened storm had arrived early. Ted and Mincer had been gone an hour, out on a job, and Sheila was at the front window fretting about them, watching leaves flying in all directions. An empty dustbin rattled and clanked down the road, coming to a juddering stop by Ted's car. He wouldn't like that, but there was nothing Sheila could do about it. She rocked back and forth in her chair. Next to her, ManyBucks stirred in his sleep, shifted his bulk, passed wind loudly and settled back down with a sibilant sigh.

A crash as the front door closed woke ManyBucks, who started barking.

'Ssh boy, ssh,' Sheila crooned. Mincer was whining and scratching in the hall. 'Get that animal into the kitchen,' Sheila shouted to her husband.

The two dogs did not get on. Sheila had told Ted it would be like that, but he had been adamant that he needed a dog like Mincer for his work.

'Terriers ferret them out like nobody's business,' he'd said. 'You couldn't to do it with a slobbery thing like a boxer.'

'Did you find it then?' Sheila said, dragging herself upright in her chair.

'Find what?'

'The body in the park that man rang about.'

'Ah, gotcha. Yes. And no. Let me get a cup of tea and then I'll tell you.'

When he came back with tea for the two of them, Ted sat down heavily. Next to Sheila, ManyBucks shifted in his sleep again.

'So, did you find it?'

Ted looked at her, twisting his mouth. In the kitchen Mincer was still whining.

'Why you doing that? And why's that animal making that noise?'

'He'll settle down in a mo.'

Ted picked up his tea and slurped it.

Sheila waited.

'Okay, we found a body, but it wasn't what we were looking for. It wasn't a rat.'

Sheila gasped and grasped the arms of her chair. 'Not a dead man?!?'

'Don't be ridiculous, woman, of course it wasn't a dead man. But– ' Ted paused and twisted his mouth again. It was– ' Ted dropped his head.

'It was what?'

'It was eviscerated.'

'E you what?'

'Eviscerated. Emptied. Just a skin and some bones left. And a bedraggled tail. Not a pretty sight.'

'Why d'you tell me that, Ted Trinket?'

'Because you asked.'

Outside the storm was getting worse. The couple sat in the room with the smelly boxer, supping their tea. The noise of the terrier in the kitchen quietened.

'So what killed it?' Sheila said eventually.

'That's what I'm wondering myself,' said Ted.

ManyBucks finds a tasty morsel

Dogs like routine. ManyBucks was no exception. He was used to seeing Sheila in her chair, or lumbering out of her chair, or settling down into it. Now there was no sign of her, but something tiny was squealing from a high shelf. ManyBucks didn't see so well. He couldn't tell what kind of thing it was, but even he with his tiny brain in a big hard skull knew that people were never that small. And it certainly didn't occur to him that this could be his mistress, Sheila, shrunken into a tiny person. No, maybe it was some kind of mouse, he thought, though he'd never seen one sitting on a shelf in the kitchen. Not to say they never did that. Just he hadn't seen it.

He sat. And he looked. And he pondered, insofar as his small brain could ponder. All the time the tiny something was squealing. It fell to the floor and lay there, quivering. ManyBucks sniffed it, experimentally licked it, opened his mouth and swallowed it.

Wild speculation

When Ted and Mincer got home and there was no sign of Sheila, Ted feared the worst, or what he thought was the worst – she must, he thought, have been miniaturised and flown off again. But there were no open windows – surely, he thought, even small Sheila couldn't fly through solid walls. Or perhaps she could... Perhaps she was responsible for the bodies that kept turning up – squirrels, mostly. This, he knew, was crazy thinking. But nothing made sense to him.

Then ManyBucks fell ill, wouldn't eat.

'You're missing your mistress, are you?' Ted said. 'Poor thing.'

He'd never liked ManyBucks, but he didn't like seeing him in pain, took him to the vet. There was a blockage, the vet said, he'd better stay in overnight. Ted tossed and turned all night, worried about Sheila, worried about her dog, worried about how worried she would be if she knew ManyBucks was ill.

The vet called next morning, early, sounding strange. 'We found something,' she said. 'You need to come in, now.'

Back again

The small body was inert.

'We've never seen anything like this before.'

Of course Ted had, but he fainted when he saw it and could not speak for some time when he came round.

'My wife,' he stuttered, eventually.

'Yes, of course, we have tried to call your wife,' said the receptionist. 'But there's no answer from your landline. Do you have a mobile number for her?'

'No, no, no, you don't understand,' he said.

'It's the shock,' said the girl, and asked again for Sheila's mobile number.

'Your wife will be here shortly,' she said, bringing him a cup of tea. 'Drink this. And eat a biscuit. You need sugar. Trust me, I know when people do; it happens a lot with animal trauma.' She nodded in what she had learnt was a manner that was generally reassuring.

Ted didn't have the strength to argue; he drank the tea, ate two chocolate biscuits, and felt slightly better. But when Sheila walked through the surgery door he fainted again.

'Don't worry me like that again, Ted Trinket,' Sheila said once they were all back home again.

'*Me*, worry *you*? It was the other way round, Sheila.' Ted's voice trailed off. He knew he was sounding pathetic again.

'It's just lucky for you my dog is okay now,' she said.

Ted decided it was best to say no more.

Off on her own

For a while Sheila went off on her own every day, in small or large form; Ted was never sure which it would be, and he didn't ask where she went. He would come home and find notes which he could only read with the aid of a magnifying glass, so small was the writing. He remonstrated with Sheila when she was back to normal, said she might at least write her messages when she was full-size. She said she'd do what she wanted, she'd kowtowed to him for long enough. Ted gave up arguing with her, out of embarrassment as much as anything, and told himself he didn't care what she did. But one day when she didn't come back and was away for days, he realised how much he wanted the old Sheila back, and for things to be as they were before. As did ManyBucks, who had suffered no lasting ill effects from his unwise ingestion, but who now set up a constant low growling which kept Ted awake at night.

The taste of freedom

When smallness came upon her Sheila was literally a different person, able to go wherever she pleased and do whatever she felt like doing – well, whatever was compatible with being a very small creature. She found her way through an open window into a playgroup for under-5s, and discovered it was fun to settle in a basket of bits and pieces and surprise the children by suddenly jumping up and buzzing around like a bee. When the helpers came to see what was exciting the children she would lie down motionless again, like any other small toy.

'It moved! It flew!' the children would cry.

'Don't be silly, it's just a little doll.' They would handle her then, those ignorant people, prod and poke her all over, and she would sting them, an ability which she discovered by chance and which gave her great pleasure. The downside was that they could drop her on the floor or even throw her across the room when that happened, and it hurt. Children would rescue her though, stroke her and kiss her, and that was comforting.

Sheila thought a lot, on those days, about how it might have been if she and Ted had had children, and discovered maternal feelings she had never experienced before, but when she returned to full size she remembered nothing of any of this. She read about her small-size exploits in the local paper, but, had she not had the premonition all those years before that this would happen, would have been inclined to think it was nothing but a story, made up to amuse people.

Amusements and dangers

Some of the things that small Sheila got up to did amuse people, especially when they spotted her flying around in places where flying things were generally not welcome. She buzzed around like an annoying fly in church, in the hairdressers, in the old people's luncheon club, in the library; there wasn't a place in Enfield small Sheila hadn't explored. When people tried to swat her she always evaded them, like most annoying flies. But, as small Sheila, she had the rather quaint ability to issue sweet nothings into the air, and that stopped people feeling annoyed, in fact made their day a little brighter.

Some things, though, she did not manage to evade. Her experience of the digestive tract of an overweight boxer dog had not been pleasant, and it was a mercy for normal-sized Sheila that she did not remember that particular part of life's journey. Small-sized Sheila remembered it all too well and from that day on she avoided getting anywhere near a dog's mouth.

Ted's burden

If those who read in the paper about Sheila's exploits were amused, her husband certainly was not. He was constantly tripping over little bits and pieces that small Sheila dropped around the house and that Mincer liked to pick up and drop in other places: small spectacles, tiny shoes, little handbags. Normal-size Sheila kept her paraphernalia neat and tidy in a basket near to the sofa where she sat, next to the bed when ManyBucks spent his days.

'Why d'you drop your stuff everywhere?' Ted would yell at his wife.

'Not me, sweet pie,' normal Sheila would retort. 'I ain't moved.'

Which was true, but small Sheila was constantly on the move.

Ted was beginning to feel as if he, like Sheila, was two different people, but unlike her he was conscious of both, and he was not happy about it, not happy at all, especially in view of the bodies.

The body situation

Ted lay awake at night thinking about bodies. There were the normal-sized bodies (most people, including Sheila much of the time), the small bodies (Sheila, and rats) and the dead bodies (rats, and other creatures). From where he stood, in the middle of the situation (alive and normal-sized) it was difficult to make sense of it all. Rats, alive or dead, he could cope with, had been doing so all his working life. With his faithful terrier alongside him sniffing out exactly where the rats were, he had no trouble dealing with them. His methods were varied – brute force and poison both played their part – and effective. He felt that he had things under control with the rats. Not so with Sheila, or the other dead bodies.

One night when Ted had been awake for hours tossing and turning, his mind going round and round in circles and getting nowhere, he dreamt, when he finally fell asleep, that small Sheila was running up and down trees with an axe, felling squirrels and then cutting them open.

In the morning it all felt ridiculous, but if Sheila's seat was empty he would still worry about where she might be, worry about what havoc she might be wreaking out in the world.

Then, her dog

Ted had never felt any affection for ManyBucks; he was Sheila's dog, and Mincer was his. The two dogs paid no attention to one another, which was a mercy, for two humans in a house squabbling was one thing, two dogs doing so definitely more trouble. In fact the dogs tended to act as peacemakers, and when Sheila retreated to her sofa sanctuary, her canine companion always settled down in his bed at her side, farting quietly.

But Sheila's excursions in miniaturised form had unsettled ManyBucks, and he started trailing after Ted round the house, which made Mincer, feeling his position under threat, snip and snap at the boxer. ManyBucks was lazy though, and made no attempt to follow when Ted and Mincer went out to work; if Sheila was not there when they returned the boxer would raise his head and utter a blood-curdling cry which made Mincer back into a corner, whimpering.

Then, a week before Christmas, things took another turn; ManyBucks went missing again, and this time he did not reappear. All the usual attempts to find a missing pet – walking the streets, calling on neighbours, contacting animal rescue centres – drew a blank. Sheila was distraught; she sat on the sofa crying all day long, as game shows blared uselessly on the TV. Ted rather wished she would fly away on one of her jaunts, even said as much to her.

'It would take your mind off it,' he said.

'You think I can just choose to become small as and when I please, do you, Ted Trinket? Well, if that's what you think, you're wrong. And, even if I could, in what way would it "take my mind off it", as you so indelicately put it? ManyBucks isn't an it; he's my baby.' She collapsed in another paroxysm of weeping.

'Sorry, sweet pea, I just thought– '

'Well, you thought wrong, and don't call me that!'

'Sorry, sorry. Sorry I spoke.' Ted crumpled into himself, backed off into the kitchen and made himself a cup of coffee. All the rats in Enfield seemed to have gone to ground, or off on their Christmas holidays; he had no work to distract him.

'Come on boy,' he said to Mincer, who was sitting patiently at his feet. 'Let's go out and have another look for the wretched hound. He has to be somewhere.'

What Ted thought, but did not dare say aloud, was that ManyBucks might have become another victim of whoever or whatever was littering Enfield with the bodies of dead animals.

Another miniaturisation

How Sheila had first turned into a small version of herself, and how she continued to do so, was a mystery. She was, of course, not the first in history, at least not the first to have been written about, though Ted wondered if all the others were just fictional.

'It's all very well in a book, but believe me in real life it's not funny, not funny at all,' he told his mates in The Square Hole.

'Can't you make some dough out of it?' said one of them.

'Dough?' Ted couldn't think straight.

'Spondulicks, cash, *money*, guv. Sell the story to the papers.'

'The papers got the story anyway. They ain't going to pay me.'

'That's just it, guv. They think it's a story, made up, like most of the garbage they print.'

Ted supped his whisky, unconvinced that his approaching any newspaperman was going to help.

It was two days before Christmas and the pub was full of a jollity that Ted did not share. He pulled on his coat and headed for the door, Mincer trotting quietly at his heels. Outside it was snowing, the flakes spinning and sparking in the lights strung in trees along the street. The snow was blowing into Ted's eyes, so he did not notice small Sheila flying past, even though she had a scarlet beret on her little head and an equally brightly coloured scarf wrapped round her tiny neck. Neither did he notice the even smaller creature flying behind her; a miniature ManyBucks, wearing a fluorescent yellow coat. The lads who had come out of the pub for a smoke saw them though, and would tell Ted when they saw him next. But this would not be until after Christmas.

Christmas Day

Sheila was cooking Christmas dinner as usual, a turkey crown for herself and Ted, a turkey leg for ManyBucks and two chicken legs for Mincer. She was in a good mood because her missing dog had reappeared that morning, snug in his bed as if delivered down the chimney by Father Christmas. She sang to herself as she peeled potatoes and parsnips, mangled versions of Christmas carols:

'Ding dong Christmas bells, away with the shepherds, hey ho the holly. Hey!' she said, realising that Ted was slouched at the table, gazing into his empty coffee mug. 'It's 12 o'clock. You not going down to the pub for a jar with your mates?'

'Nah,' he mumbled.

'You feeling okay?'

'Yeah,' was all he would say.

Sheila shrugged and started chopping the veg with a vigorous action. Ted didn't move, in spite of the close proximity of the flailing knife.

'You sure you're okay?'

'I'm fine. Don't fuss.'

'And a very merry Christmas to you too, Ted Trinket. I've a good mind to go out myself and leave you to get the dinner on the table.'

'No, no, no, NO!' Ted sprang to his feet, Mincer started dancing round his ankles and from the front room came the unmistakable sound of ManyBucks wheezing his way towards the kitchen.

'Whoa!' cried Sheila, dropping her knife, which landed tip down between two floorboards as if aimed there, quivering mere millimetres from Ted's right foot. 'Calm down, all of you,' she yelled.

Ted flopped back onto his chair. Mincer turned round twice and sank to the floor, chin stuck out defiantly, eyes darting back and forth between Ted and Sheila, while ManyBucks slowly turned tail, emitted a loud and exceptionally smelly fart and lumbered back into the living room.

'For goodness sake.' Sheila mopped her brow with a tea-towel. 'Now, please tell me what the matter is.' She sat down herself opposite her husband, and raised a quizzical eyebrow. 'Is it the cardigan?'

26

'The cardigan is perfect,' he said. He leant down and pulled the knife out from between the floorboards.

'You don't mean it. You hate the colour.'

'I do. I don't. I mean I don't hate the colour. You're confusing me.' He ran his right index finger along the blade of the knife.

(He did hate the colour; men, in his trade and in his pub, did not wear turquoise cardigans.)

'You're lying. And look what you've done, you idiot!'

Blood was dripping from Ted's right index finger, large bright drops landing on the floorboards.

Sheila saw red, literally and metaphorically, and her good mood evaporated; she untied her apron, pulled it over her head and flung it to the ground. Ted screwed his eyes tight shut, not wanting to see what he was convinced would happen next.

'I've had enough of your nonsense, Ted Trinket! I'm off!'

When Ted opened his eyes there was no sign of Sheila, large or small. Neither did he hear the creak and squeak of the front door opening and shutting. Outside, it was snowing again. If there had been any footprints leading away from the house, they were now obscured. All the windows were shut, but this had not stopped small Sheila flying away before.

Ted was not in a fit state to try and understand what had happened to his wife. He wrapped a piece of kitchen paper round his bleeding finger, went into the living room, turned on the TV and poured himself a large glass of whisky. After the third whisky the depression where Sheila normally sat seemed to be pulsating, but his finger was no longer hurting. He got up, walked unsteadily into the kitchen and replaced the blood-soaked paper with a clean piece. The uncooked vegetables, some of which had spots of blood on them, seemed to be glaring at him, but the turkey was cooked, albeit rather dry. He divided half the crown between himself and the two dogs and they fell upon it like starving travellers. Afterward, all three of them slept, as the television blared through the afternoon, the snow continued to fall and Sheila did not return.

The day after Boxing Day

Afterwards, Ted was unable to remember anything about Boxing Day. He assumed he had slept through it. He was certainly very hungry when he woke on the following day. He was surprised that the dogs had not woken him, though less surprised when he saw the oven door ajar, the empty baking dishes and the turkey and chicken bones on the kitchen floor.

At The Square Hole the lads were in jovial mood, all glad to be freed of family bonds.

'Good Christmas Ted?' one of them said, but got only a glare in response.

After a few beers he felt better, or at least more combative, and able to josh with the lads about flighty spouses. 'You say you saw my Sheila flying along the road before Christmas. Maybe so, but what about your missus, Dave, and yours, Mike – they get up to mischief too, I'll be bound.'

What Ted didn't know until they told him was about ManyBucks being miniaturised too.

'The boxer? Flying? Wearing a yellow coat? You sure? How much had you all had to drink?'

His mates nodded solemnly and said they were sure, and for all that they then fell about laughing, Ted knew by this time that fact was far stranger than fiction, so he just shook his head, knowing there was nothing he could say, or do, to change things.

Sorting out the bodies

Afterwards, when everything had settled down, Ted could see that he'd got things out of proportion with the bodies. He knew that rats killed squirrels and other small mammals, so getting rid of the rats was obviously the answer. Somehow things had got out of balance; he didn't know how or why.

By the summer after the awful Christmas things were back to normal for his business. In fact it was thriving, because there'd been so much in the press about what had happened to Ted's wife, and her dog. People did feel sorry for Ted, and many felt the least they could do was pass on word about his business, not just in Enfield, but beyond, because it turned out he was the last rat-catcher in the whole of the county.

There would never be any way of stopping rats breeding in the sewers, but if and when they ventured into people's houses Ted Trinket, now known as Torcie (the Only Rat-Catcher in Essex), was the man for the job, and, with the help of his faithful terrier, did a good job dispatching them.

The way things went on

Ted's business might have been thriving, but for Sheila life remained a story of two halves; for all that she appeared to her husband to be content sitting watching the TV and doing her crafting with her faithful hound – also content – by her side, both of them took off from time to time on excursions in miniature form, sometimes together, sometimes separately. They were a common sight around Enfield and local people stopped remarking on them, though Ted's mates in the pub did come out with the odd jibe:

'Your missus up to her old tricks again, is she?'

He refused to be drawn, but remarks like that did make him feel small himself, and he sometimes wished that he could fly off on a jaunt too, and said as much to Mincer, who barked in response as if to say he thought the same.

Completion

It was a whole year before it stopped, but stop it finally did. No more miniaturisation of woman or dog, no more sad depressions in the sofa and the dog-bed in the living room.

There'd been a point in the saga when Ted thought he would have been relieved if Sheila took off with the milkman again, but he realised this was impractical, neither Sheila nor Derek the milkman being in the first flush or in all probability up to it, even if they wanted to be.

To the questions why and how things had happened as they did, Ted had no answers; he was simply glad that life had settled down again, and, so it seemed, was Sheila. They had never wanted children, but now, for the first time, they talked about getting a cat, a shared pet.

'But what about the dogs?' said Ted.

'They'll cope,' said Sheila.

Which they did and more. When, with the blessing the local cat rescue service, an ever-purring cuddly ball of white fur called Scheherazade came to live with them, she made the Trinket home complete and, finally, peaceful, because Sheila, Ted, Mincer and ManyBucks all fell in love with her.

And after that there was no more of any of them being small ever again, or even feeling small.

Acknowledgements

This work was longlisted in the Bath Novella-in-Flash Award 2025.

Many thanks to Thomas Thomas and LeAnne Hunt for editorial support.

Nancy Stohlman, for curating the prompts for Flash Nano 2023, where Sheila's story had its genesis.

Alison May, for her superb workshop on Planning and Pantsing, where the story began to take off.

And thanks, always, to Oliver and Feely for listening and sticking with me.

Biography

Cath Barton's novella *The Plankton Collector* was the winner of the AmeriCymru Prize for the Novella in 2017, published by New Welsh Rarebyte in 2018 and republished by Parthian in 2025.

The Miniaturisation of Sheila Trinket is her fifth published novella, following *In the Sweep of the Bay* (Louise Walters Books, 2020), *The Geography of the Heart* (Arroya Seco Press, 2023), and *Between the Virgin and the Sea* (Leamington Books, 2023). Her pamphlet of short stories *Mr Bosch and His Owls* was published by Atomic Bohemian in 2024. She also writes flash fiction and is working on a novel set in the circus.

She lives in Wales and is a keen hill-walker.

A whimsical glimpse at the ups and downs of married life.

—Charmaine Wilkerson, Author, Bath Flash Fiction Novella-in-Flash Award-Winning *How to Make a Window Snake.*

Told in bite-size chapters that make for a fast and fun read, *The Miniaturization of Sheila Trinket* is a total delight – to everyone but her long-suffering husband, Tim Trinket. Their decades-long marriage, settled into boredom and bickering, is upended when Sheila begins inexplicably shrinking to the size of a fly and setting off on adventures that have Tim combing the county looking for her. I easily read this charming tale in one sitting and loved it.

–Jayne Martin, author *Tender Cuts* Vine Leaves Press

Sheila and Ted Trinket have their separate lives. He is down the pub when he's not following his profession as a rat catcher with his dog, Mincer. She is at home crafting and watching TV with her 'malodorous' bull dog, ManyBucks. Everything changes when Sheila suddenly miniaturises to the size of a bee and has the ability to fly. It takes this for Ted to pay attention. He'd ignored Sheila's affair with another man many years before. But bewildered and then distraught, he can't ignore this. Cath Barton is a very inventive writer, and portrays the main characters and their lives vividly and also with humour and compassion. We never learn quite why Sheila develops magical powers which come and go, but it's satisfying to see them as a metaphor for a woman freeing herself in a stuck and lonely relationship, then finding a resolution with her husband at the end.

—Jude Higgins

www.ingramcontent.com/pod-product-compliance
Lightning Source LLC
Chambersburg PA
CBHW051515260626
47162CB00008B/2984